Developing Reader titles are ide… …nfidently using their phonics knowl… …entences with only a little help. Freq… …ve fluency and confidence.

Special features:

Short, simple sentences

Frequent repetition of main words and phrases

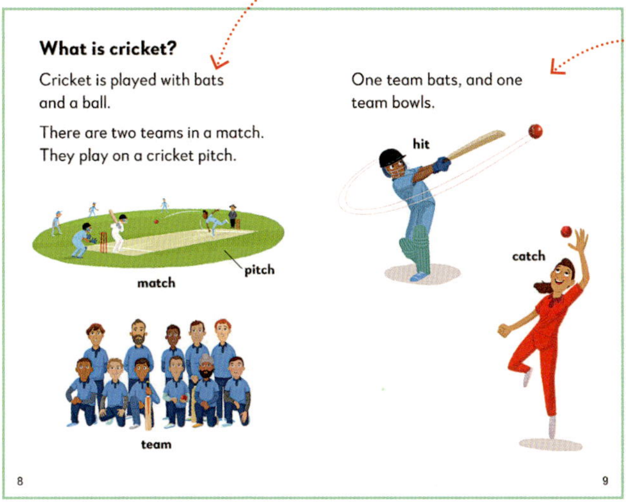
What is cricket?

Cricket is played with bats and a ball.

There are two teams in a match. They play on a cricket pitch.

One team bats, and one team bowls.

Careful match between text and pictures

Large, clear type

How to score

When a team is batting, this is called their innings.

They can score runs when it is their innings.

The batting player hits the ball.

They run to the other wicket to score a run.

18 19

Ladybird

Educational Consultants: Geraldine Taylor and James Clements
Book Banding Consultant: Kate Ruttle
Subject Consultant: Clive Gifford

LADYBIRD BOOKS

UK | USA | Canada | Ireland | Australia
India | New Zealand | South Africa

Ladybird Books is part of the Penguin Random House group of companies
whose addresses can be found at global.penguinrandomhouse.com.

www.penguin.co.uk www.puffin.co.uk www.ladybird.co.uk

Penguin Random House UK

First published 2018
This edition published 2025
001

Written by Sasha Morton

Illustrations by John Lund

Printed in Dubai

The authorized representative in the EEA is Penguin Random House Ireland,
Morrison Chambers, 32 Nassau Street, Dublin D02 YH68

A CIP catalogue record for this book is available from the British Library

ISBN: 978-0-241-67304-1

All correspondence to:
Ladybird Books
Penguin Random House Children's
One Embassy Gardens, 8 Viaduct Gardens, London SW11 7BW

MIX
Paper | Supporting responsible forestry
FSC® C018179

Read It Yourself

I'm a Cricketer

Written by Sasha Morton
Illustrated by John Lund

Contents

What is cricket?

Cricket is played with bats and a ball.

There are two teams in a match. They play on a cricket pitch.

One team bats, and one team bowls.

The cricket team

There are eleven players in a cricket team.

Out of the eleven players, some players are best at bowling, and some are best at batting.

The cricket kit

This is a cricket kit.

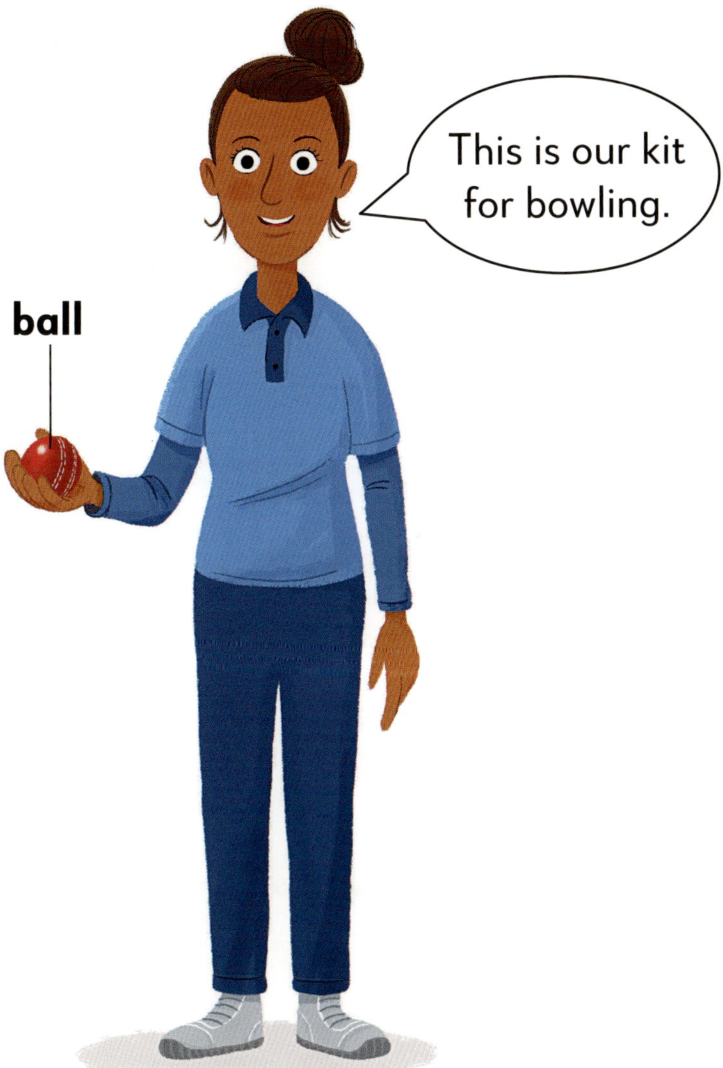
This is our kit
for bowling.
ball

Where to play

This is where the two teams of eleven play cricket. It is called the pitch.

BAT 4
44
OVERS 32
174
5
BAT 7
9
I am batting.

How to play cricket

This is a cricket match.

The bowler bowls the ball.

The batting player hits the ball with the bat.

Other players, called fielders, run to catch the ball.

How to score

When a team is batting, this is called their innings.

They can score runs when it is their innings.

The batting player hits the ball.

They run to the other wicket to score a run.

Bowling

This team is bowling.

If the ball hits the wicket, the batting player is out!

Batting

Now, this team is batting.
It is their innings.

They try to score more runs than the other team.

How to get players out

Players on the bowling team try to hit the wicket with the ball.

Players can catch the batting player out, too.

How to win

A team wins a match if they score more runs than the other team.

BAT 10
6
OVERS 47
247
9
BAT 11
4
You did well!
You did well, too!

Picture glossary

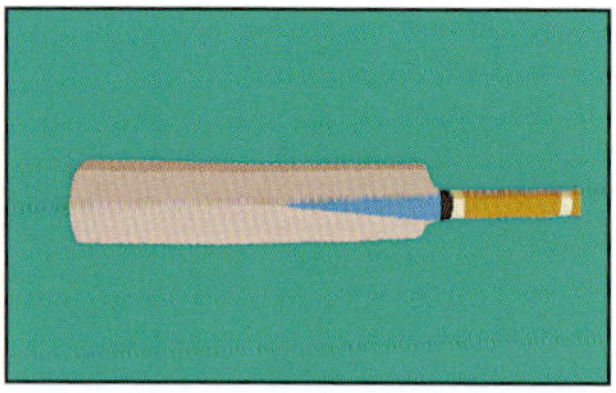

bat

bowl

catch

cricketer

hit

kit

match

players

team

wicket

Index

I'm a cricketer quiz

What have you learned about cricketers? Answer these questions and find out!

- How many players are there in a cricket team?
- What do cricketers use to hit the ball?
- How does a team win a match?